**DO NOT REMOVE
CARDS FROM POCKET**

4/97

**ALLEN COUNTY PUBLIC LIBRARY
FORT WAYNE, INDIANA 46802**

You may return this book to any agency, branch,

or bookmobile of the Allen County Public Library.

DEMCO

HOW-TO SPORTS

GYMNASTICS

Paul Joseph
ABDO & Daughters

Published by Abdo & Daughters, 4940 Viking Drive, Suite 622, Edina, Minnesota 55435.

Copyright © 1996 by Abdo Consulting Group, Inc., Pentagon Tower, P.O. Box 36036, Minneapolis, Minnesota 55435 USA. International copyrights reserved in all countries. No part of this book may be reproduced in any form without written permission from the publisher.

Printed in the United States.

Cover Photo credits: Allsport
Interior Photo credits: Superstock, pages 17, 18, 21, 22, 24
　　　　　　　　　　Allsport, pages 5, 7, 9, 26

Edited by Bob Italia

Library of Congress Cataloging-in-Publication Data

Joseph, Paul, 1970-
　　Gymnastics / Paul Joseph
　　　p. cm. -- (How-To-Sports)
　　Includes index.
　　Summary: Gives a basic introduction to gymnastics, including a brief history of the sport and descriptions of essential exercises.
　　　ISBN 1-56239-648-X
　　1. Gymnastics--Juvenile literature. [1. Gymnastics.] I. Title. II. Series:
　　GV461.J78 1996　　　　　　　　　　　　　　　　　　　96-13487
　　796.44--dc20　　　　　　　　　　　　　　　　　　　　　　CIP
　　　　　　　　　　　　　　　　　　　　　　　　　　　　　　　AC

Contents

The Exciting Sport of Gymnastics

Gymnastics is very popular with young boys and girls throughout the world. Gymnasts must be able to perform physical activities that require **balance**, strength, and body control. But more importantly, a person must be strong mentally, concentrating at all times.

Imagine yourself running at full-speed and doing a **front handspring**, or standing on a 4-inch (10-cm) wide piece of wood and performing a **back-flip**. Because it takes so much skill, many people love watching this challenging sport.

Gymnastics takes a lot of practice and training. But if you like excitement and a true challenge, this is the sport for you.

Gymnastics is a very physical sport.

How Gymnastics Started

Gymnastics has been around for thousands of years. Many believe it was started by the **Greeks**. But the sport gained popularity when Friedrich Jahn of **Germany** formed the first gymnastics club in 1811.

Jahn built an outdoor gymnastics center. He made his equipment with anything he could find. With this homemade equipment, he taught students different moves and developed their strength.

Gymnastics became very popular throughout the world. By the time the first modern **Olympics** took place in 1896, it was one of the nine original sports.

In the 1896 **Olympics**, only men participated. But in 1928, the women's gymnastics competition was introduced. By the 1970s, female gymnasts had become more famous than male gymnasts.

Recently, women have dominated the sport of gymnastics.

Getting Started

Anyone can learn gymnastics, but it is best to begin at an early age. Many of the best gymnasts started as early as three years old.

When learning, a gymnast will work on **coordination**, **balance**, and **flexibility**. A gymnast must be naturally flexible and strong. Beginning gymnasts work on pointing their toes and stretching their muscles. Much of the time is devoted to learning **tumbling** skills.

After gymnasts learn tumbling skills, they will begin working on the **apparatus**. The apparatus is the equipment used in the events, such as the **uneven parallel bars**, **horizontal bar**, **rings**, **pommel horse**, **vault**, **parallel bars**, and **balance beam**.

A gymnast practicing on the balance beam.

The Workout

Gymnastics takes a lot of hard work and practice. A gymnast will go over his or her routine many times, putting in many hours. This practice is called a workout.

Most workouts include three parts: the warm-up, **apparatus** practice, and **conditioning**. The warm-up is the most important because it helps prevent injuries. During the warm-up, gymnasts stretch and flex their entire body. Most warm-ups take place on a floor mat where teammates can help each other.

After the warm-up, gymnasts divide into smaller groups. The coach sets the workout time for each apparatus, and the gymnasts start their practice. When their time is up, the gymnasts rotate to the next **apparatus**. At the end of the entire rotation, each gymnast will go to the apparatus that he or she competes on and work extra hard.

At the end of the warm-up, gymnasts finish with **conditioning**. They may do sit-ups, splits, push-ups, and sprints to increase strength, **endurance**, and **flexibility**.

The Events

Boys and girls gymnastics events look a lot alike. In many gymnastics classes, boys and girls can learn some of the same skills.

There are six events in boys gymnastics: **floor exercise**, **vault**, **pommel horse**, **parallel bars**, **horizontal bar**, and **rings**. Girls compete in four: floor exercise, vault, **uneven parallel bars**, and **balance beam**.

After beginners practice each event for many hours, they will discover the event that is best suited for them. A coach also can help them select the right event.

Boys Events

The **floor exercise** gives gymnasts a limited amount of time to perform their routine. The routine is judged on how well each gymnast uses strength, control, power, and precision.

Gymnasts perform the floor exercise on a floor that has springs mounted under a layer of wood. Another thick layer of foam is placed on top of the wood. A 40 x 40-foot (12 x 12-meter) piece of carpet is put on top of the foam.

The **vault** is a padded wooden structure nearly 4 feet (1 m) high. A **springboard** is placed in front of the vault. A long, cushioned runway leads to the springboard.

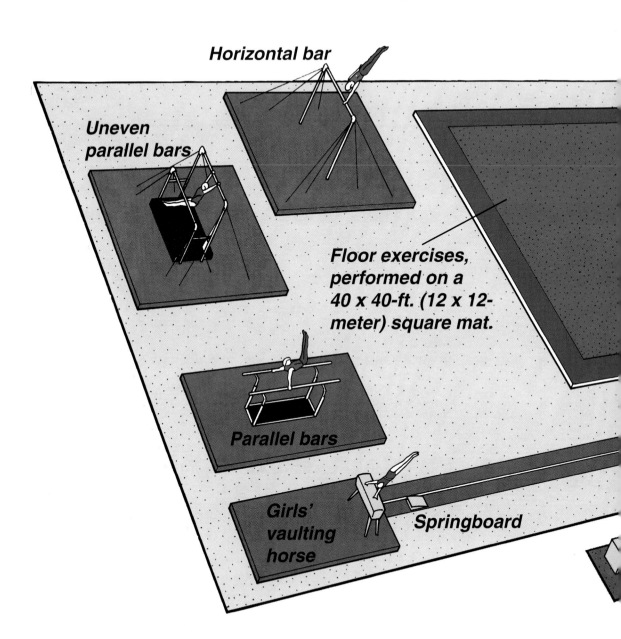

Horizontal bar

Uneven parallel bars

Floor exercises, performed on a 40 x 40-ft. (12 x 12-meter) square mat.

Parallel bars

Girls' vaulting horse

Springboard

14

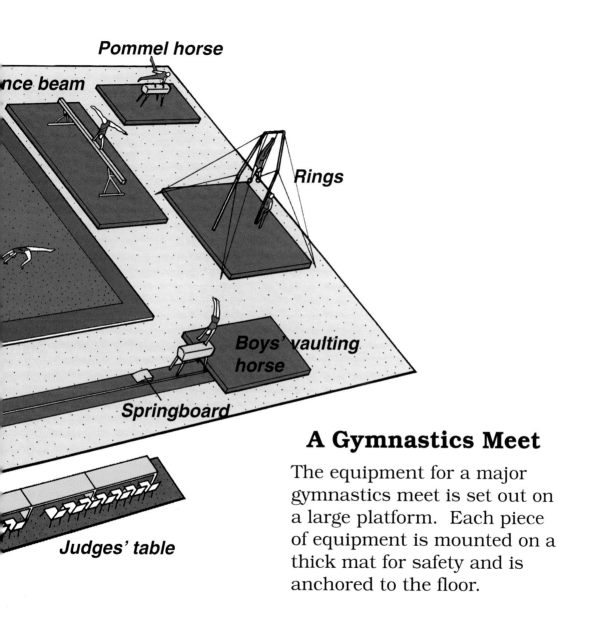

Pommel horse

nce beam

Rings

Boys' vaulting horse

Springboard

Judges' table

A Gymnastics Meet

The equipment for a major gymnastics meet is set out on a large platform. Each piece of equipment is mounted on a thick mat for safety and is anchored to the floor.

The main object of the **vault** is to run as fast as possible on the runway, push off the **springboard**, and touch the vault for a split-second. This will get the gymnast into the air where flips and twists are performed before landing on a padded mat. Each gymnast is judged on speed, control, difficulty, and landing.

The **pommel horse** looks much like the vault and is the same size. But it also has two handles on top called pommels.

In this event, gymnasts use the pommels to support their weight while swinging side to side and forward to backward. This takes a lot of strength and practice. The event is judged according to difficulty and form.

The pommel horse.

The parallel bars.

The **parallel bars** are two bars that are exactly even. They are 5.5 feet (1.5 m) above the ground, about 1.5 feet (.5 m) apart, and 11.5 feet (3.5 m) long.

The gymnast must position the body between the bars, grab them with both hands, and lift the body from the floor. Then the gymnast can swing the legs over the bars and keep the routine flowing. Most of the movements are done above the bars. The routine is judged on performance, difficulty, and **dismount**.

The **horizontal bar** is an 8-foot-long (2.5-meter-long) steel bar placed about 8 feet (2.5 m) above the floor. The gymnast will usually hold on with two hands—but sometimes use only one. The object is to swing the body around many times.

The final part of the routine is the **dismount**. It usually includes one or two flips, and is judged closely.

The **rings** are around 1.5 feet (.46 m) apart and hang over 8 feet (2.5 m) above the ground. Made of wood, they are completely circular and suspended by straps from a steel frame.

In the routine, the gymnasts perform circle and swinging movements. They also will stop and hold themselves in different positions to show control.

Because the rings hang loosely, a gymnast who performs on the rings needs plenty of arm strength. Otherwise, he cannot hold his body still during his routine.

Opposite page:
The rings require plenty
of arm strength.

A gymnast with her coach preparing for a floor exercise.

Girls Events

The **floor exercise** is an event where girls are given 90 seconds to perform their routine. This routine must have a combination of dancing and **tumbling**. It also must be **choreographed** to music.

Gymnasts are judged on technique. Pointed toes and near perfect body line is very important.

The girls **vault** event is similar to the boys event. The girls vault is placed sideways on the floor rather than lengthwise.

Gymnasts spring off a board after running down the runway. While in the air, gymnasts can do a number of routines, from flips to twists. The **dismount** is very important. The judges watch for movement after the landing is performed.

A gymnast performs on the uneven parallel bars.

The **uneven parallel bars** are 2 bars, 8 feet (2.5 m) long. One bar is 7.5 feet (2.2 m) above the floor and the other is nearly 5 feet (1.5 m) high.

This event takes the skill of the **parallel bars**—then adds an even more difficult dimension with the **horizontal bar**. The object is to continually swing and circle the body while going from one bar to the next. It is also important to finish with a strong **dismount**.

The **balance beam** is made of wood that has a padded, suede covering. It is 4 inches (10 cm) wide and 16.5 feet (5 m) long. The beam is nearly 4 feet (1.2 m) above the floor.

A balance beam routine is 90 seconds long. It begins when the gymnast leaves the floor to get on the beam. The gymnast must show **balance** while posing, dancing, and **tumbling**. Some gymnasts even do flips!

A gymnast performing on the balance beam.

To end the routine, the gymnast **dismounts**, which is judged just as heavily as any of the moves performed on the beam.

Fair Play and Team Spirit

Gymnastics has much to offer. It is a sport that girls and boys can enjoy. And though gymnasts perform individually, gymnastics is also a team sport.

Because gymnastics is so difficult, you must always be confident. Cheer, encourage, and help your teammates no matter how they perform their routine. Congratulate opponents when they perform well, too.

Once you learn the basics, join a club at your school or in your community. Then you will see why gymnastics is so popular throughout the world.

Glossary

apparatus (ap-uh-RAT-us) - The equipment used in the gymnastics events.

back-flip - Jumping up in the air and rotating yourself in a circular motion backwards and landing on your feet.

balance - A steady condition or position that you hold your body in.

balance beam - A beam 4 inches (10 cm) wide and 16.5 feet (4.5 m) long on which girls perform timed routines.

choreograph (KORE-e-oh-graff) - Different routines arranged to music.

conditioning (kun-DISH-un-ing) - The use of exercise to make the body healthy and strong.

coordination (koe-or-dih-NAY-shun) - Physically acting in a smooth way.

dismount (DIS-mownt)- The way in which the gymnast leaves the apparatus after the routine is finished. It is also the final move of the routine.

endurance (en-DER-ants) - The ability to withstand physical activity.

flexibility (flex-uh-BILL-uh-tee) - Able to move yourself in many different positions and not be stiff.

floor exercise - A timed gymnastics event performed on a mat measuring 40 x 40 feet (12 x 12 m). Both boys and girls compete in this event.

front handspring - A forward jump onto the gymnast's hands with immediate rotation forward onto their feet.

Germany - A country in central Europe where gymnastics is to have gained popularity and made into the sport it is today.

Greeks - People born or living in Greece, who started the sport of gymnastics thousands of years ago.

horizontal bar - A bar supported by poles where boys perform their routine.

Olympics (oh-LIM-piks) - Athletic contests held every two years in a different country. Athletes from many nations compete in them.

parallel bars - A pair of bars of the same height and parallel to each other on which boys do their routines.

pommel horse - A leather-covered frame that has two handles. It looks much like the vault. Boys perform routines on this apparatus.

rings - A pair of stationary rings supported from ropes and straps on which boys perform their routines.

springboard - A springy board used in jumping or vaulting.

tumbling - To perform leaps, somersaults, or other acrobatic tricks in gymnastics.

uneven parallel bars - A pair of bars that are parallel to each other but one is higher than the other. Girls perform their routine on this apparatus.

vault - A flat-surfaced, leather-covered rectangular structure on supports, that both girls and boys use for routines. But girls use it sideways while boys use it lengthwise.

Index